# A Note from PJ Library®

## You're Welcome

There's a new kid in Max's class, and Max isn't sure he likes her. It takes a spin back in time for Max to learn that *hachnasat orchim* (Hebrew for "welcoming guests") is among the most prized of Jewish values. As it says in *Pirkei Avot* (*Ethics of the Ancestors*, a collection of rabbinic sayings): "Find yourself a teacher, acquire for yourself a friend, and judge everyone in a positive light." When Max decides to look for Emma's good qualities, he acquires for himself a new friend. Seems like he also found himself some teachers—in the form of ancient biblical characters! To learn more, visit pjlibrary.org/maxbuildsatimemachine.

## Angels 101

Angels are peppered throughout the Torah (the first five books of the Bible), and rabbinic commentaries include lots of discussions about them. One common idea is that while we humans enjoy free will and can pursue many goals, angels can only pursue one mission that has been assigned to them by God. Their entire identity is bound up in that one mission. If that's the case, the angels in this story would appear to be charged with testing Abraham and Sarah's hospitality. As Max sees, Abraham and Sarah pass their test with flying colors.

## An Ancient Question

"Mrs. Mooshky," asks Max, "do you think there were any angels when God split the Red Sea?" Believe it or not, Max is not the first person to wonder about this—the ancient rabbis did, too. And like Max, they also had active imaginations, picturing God and the angels debating whether to punish the Egyptians for enslaving the Israelites. Different angels had differing opinions, but of course, it was God's decision in the end—and God did indeed punish the Egyptians, but also forbade anyone from celebrating that. Any other questions, Max?

## Talk It Over

As you read this story, ask yourself some questions:

How does Max feel about Emma at the start of this story compared to the end? Why do his feelings change?

How are Max and Emma similar, and how are they different? How are you and your friends similar and different?

If you could travel back in time, where would you want to go?

## Try It Out!

Sarah and Abraham are models of hospitality that we can all learn from. Consider creating a special placemat for visitors. All you need is a large piece of poster board and basic art supplies. Decorate the poster board however you like, including a message like "I'm Glad You're Here." You can do this before your friend arrives, or make it a fun activity to work on together before a snack!

# Max Builds a
# Time Machine

by Carl Harris Shuman

illustrated by C.B. Decker

For my wife, Beth.
 — C.H.S.

To my brother, Jon, who knows the truth about cardboard boxes!
 — C.B.D.

*A midrash is a creative retelling of a Torah story. Rooted in love for the story itself, a good midrash helps us reimagine biblical characters and explore what we can learn from them. This book is a midrash that uses humor to expand on the story of how the first Jews, Abraham and Sarah, welcomed three rather unusual visitors. The commandment to be kind to people who are different appears more than any other commandment in the Torah and is a central theme of this book.*

Apples & Honey Press
An Imprint of Behrman House Publishers
Millburn, New Jersey 07041
www.applesandhoneypress.com

Text copyright © 2022 by Carl Harris Shuman
Illustrations copyright © 2022 by C.B. Decker
ISBN 978-1-68115-568-5

Library of Congress Cataloging-in-Publication Data
Names: Shuman, Carl Harris, author. | Decker, C. B., illustrator.
Title: Max builds a time machine / by Carl Harris Shuman, CB Decker.
Description: Millburn, New Jersey : Apples & Honey Press, [2022] | Series:
   [Max and Emma ; book 1] | Summary: "Max, a kid with a big imagination,
   builds a time machine to meet Abraham, Sarah, and three mysterious
   angels in biblical times"-- Provided by publisher.
Identifiers: LCCN 2020044401 | ISBN 9781681155685 (hardcover)
Subjects: LCSH: Bible. Old Testament--History of Biblical events--Juvenile
   fiction. | CYAC: Bible. Old Testament--History of Biblical
   events--Fiction. | Time travel--Fiction. | Angels--Fiction. | Abraham
   (Biblical patriarch)--Fiction. | Sarah (Biblical matriarch)--Fiction. |
   Jews--Fiction.
Classification: LCC PZ7.1.S51813 Max 2022 | DDC [E]--dc23
LC record available at https://lccn.loc.gov/2020044401

The illustrations in this book were created using a combination of traditional and digital tools.

Designed by Susan and David Neuhaus/NeuStudio
Edited by Alef Davis
Printed in China

9  8  7  6  5  4  3  2  1

0622/B1881/A7

# Chapter 1

# Max Gets an Idea

Mrs. Mooshky was not Max's favorite teacher. For one thing, she had a squeaky voice that Max found irritating. For another, she smelled like peppermint, which made Max sneeze when she walked past his desk. Max also thought she asked too many questions, especially of him.

"So, children, yesterday we learned that God told Abraham to leave his home and go to Canaan, where he and Sarah built a big tent. Does anyone know what the Torah says about the mysterious strangers who visited them? Max?"

Max knew that Abraham and Sarah were sort of like the mom and dad of the Jewish people—but he knew nothing about their visitors. Would the class laugh at him if he guessed and gave the wrong answer? At first he pretended he was invisible. When that didn't work, he slumped in his chair, lowered his head, and studied his new light-up sneakers.

Emma, however, was quick to wave her hand and pop out of her chair. "Ooh! Ooh! I know! I know!"

Max found Emma a little annoying. She had only just moved to town. Why did she have to know everything?

Emma had freckles and frizzy red hair. She hummed a lot, even during class. Plus, she wore pink sneakers and a floppy pink hat with a flower. Because she was new to the class and a little different from the other kids, no one talked to her much.

"So, Emma, what can you tell us about the strangers?" Mrs. Mooshky asked.

"Well, there were three of them," Emma said. "And they were really angels—but Abraham and Sarah didn't know that. So, thinking the angels were just human beings, Sarah and Abraham welcomed them by washing the strangers' feet and serving them tuna fish on rye bread! Feeding tuna on rye to strangers is a good way to make them feel at home."

"Tuna fish? I'm not sure about that part," Mrs. Mooshky said. "But you're right, Emma. Abraham and Sarah understood that it's important to welcome people we don't know—"

"And wash their feet!" Emma said.

Max scrunched his face. Washing an angel's dirty feet? Yuck!

Eitan was playing with a small plastic airplane under his desk. He raised his hand.

"Yes, Eitan," Mrs. Mooshky said.

"I don't get it," Eitan said. "How come Abraham didn't know they were angels? Where were their wings?"

"What do you think?" Mrs. Mooshky asked.

"Well, maybe their wings were detachable, like this airplane's." Eitan made several explosion sounds and snapped the wings off his toy.

Max rolled his eyes.

"I think they were like Transformers!" Emma blurted out. "You know, like cars that turn into robots."

This time, Max rolled his eyes *and* gritted his teeth.

"Those are all . . . um . . . *interesting* ideas," Mrs. Mooshky said. "And speaking of which, did you know that some rabbis say the angels only pretended to eat the food that Abraham and Sarah gave them? Why do you think some rabbis believe that?"

"Because angels aren't people and can't eat food like us!" Emma shouted. "Personally, I would not like to be an angel if I couldn't eat a good tuna fish sandwich. Of course, if there's too much mayonnaise, that's a different story."

Max placed his head on his desk and groaned. If God can create angels, he thought, God can make it possible for them to eat people food. Max was sure that Emma had it all wrong.

He looked out the window. "If only I could go back in time and see what angels were like for myself," he mumbled.

That gave Max an idea.

# Chapter 2

## Max Is No Angel

**M**ax was looking forward to art class with Ms. Quimby, who hardly asked any questions and who smelled normal. A few markers and construction paper were all Max would need to design a time machine. But first it was time for lunch.

In the cafeteria, Emma sat across from Max and began to eat her tuna fish sandwich.

"Nice sneakers," she said.

Max kicked the leg of the table so that his sneaker flashed yellow and green. Emma giggled.

"Why do you wear big floppy hats?" Max asked.

"Because they make me feel taller."

"Why do you hum?"

"Because they don't let you sing at the top of your lungs when you walk down the hall. Do you know how to hum?"

Max began to whistle.

"No, *hum*, silly. Not whistle," Emma said, laughing.

Max frowned.

"Do you honestly think angels are Transformers who can't eat tuna fish?" he asked.

"I think so," she said. "Then again, I don't actually know any angels. Do you?"

Max fiddled with his Power Patrol lunch box. "Are you making fun of me?"

"No," Emma said. "I mean, is there some law that says angels exist only in the Bible? For all I know, you could be one."

Max removed the cream cheese and olive sandwich from his lunch box and took a large bite. Then he opened his mouth.

"See?" he said. "I'm chewing. Now I'm swallowing. No angel."

"Ewww, that's gross!" Emma began to blow milk bubbles through her straw. When she giggled, she accidentally sucked some milk up her nose and had a coughing fit.

"See? I'm no angel either," she said, wiping milk from her face with her sleeve.

Max had never met anyone like Emma. He wasn't sure it was safe to be her friend. What would the other kids think if they saw them together? Max decided that it probably wasn't worth the risk.

Emma, however, had other plans.

In art class, she hovered over Max while he was drawing his time machine. "What's that? It looks like a small spaceship."

Max hunched over his drawing.

"Well, *is* it a spaceship?"

"Excuse me," Max said, "but are you always this nosy?"

Emma smiled. "Oh, yes! In fact, it's one of my best qualities. My mother also says I have my head in the clouds and stars in my eyes, which probably explains why I like using my telescope."

"You're kind of weird."

Max thought he saw a tear as Emma returned to her desk.

Max felt badly about insulting Emma, but he had important things to do. He had to go home and build a time machine so that he could find out what angels were really like.

# Chapter 3
# Building a Time Machine

**M**ax liked to build things out of cardboard boxes. He had already created a cardboard racing car and a cardboard helicopter. Max was a big believer in cardboard transportation.

As soon as he got home, Max ran to his room, placed his drawing from art class on the floor, and began to build his time machine. He filled a large, sturdy, cardboard box with old pillows to make comfy seats. He created a console from his drone control board, and a steering wheel from his old tricycle handlebars. Finally, he built an engine from a motorized Erector Set that his parents had given him for Hanukkah.

Max was proud of his latest invention. He realized, however, that he needed something to help his machine go back in time. So he went downstairs to the kitchen to find his mom. She was taking a freshly baked challah out of the oven and was covered in flour.

"Mom," he asked, "do you have an old phone you're not using?"

"Why?" she asked. "The last time I lent you something, the beaters from my electric mixer somehow became your helicopter propellers."

"I need it for one of my secret experiments."

Max's mom looked in the family junk drawer. "Aha! I knew it was here somewhere. How about my old smartphone? It doesn't make calls anymore, but the Siri function still works. Does that help?"

Max ran upstairs with his prize, closed his bedroom door, looked for his Mr. Fixit tool set (which was buried underneath a pile of underwear), and reprogrammed Siri to become "Miri," the world's smartest phone.

"Max, time for Shabbat dinner!" his mother yelled from the kitchen.

"Darn!" Max tinkered with Miri's "on" button. "I just need a few more minutes—"

"A minute equals sixty seconds. According to my calculations, it is now four minutes—or 240 seconds—before sundown, eastern standard time."

"Miri? . . . Eureka! You work!"

"Of course I work," Miri said. "But it is almost Shabbat, the day of rest. In 220 seconds I'll go into sleep mode. Come back Sunday morning. Goodbye!"

"Goodbye?" Max yelled, shaking Miri. "How can I wait until Sunday?"

As hard as he tried, Max couldn't rest on Shabbat. Not only did he spill grape juice all over his parents' white tablecloth on Friday night, he dropped his prayer book *twice* during junior congregation on Saturday morning and accidentally dumped the spice box on the floor during Saturday night's *havdalah* service.

On Sunday morning, Max went into hyperdrive. He put on his Power Patrol costume from Purim, his red cape, his X-ray goggles, and his light-up sneakers. Then he stepped into his time machine and said Hamotzi, the blessing for bread, which was one of the few prayers he knew by heart. He figured that God would understand and rearrange the Hebrew letters into something more suitable for a boy who had just invented a time machine. After he said "amen," Max pressed Miri's "on" button and held his breath.

"Hello, Max," Miri said. "Did you have a restful Shabbat?"

"Not exactly," Max said. "Did you?"

"Yes, I recharged during Shabbat, and I am now ready for anything," Miri replied. "It is a lovely day, 68 degrees Fahrenheit, 20 degrees Celsius, with a brisk ten-mile-per-hour breeze coming out of the northeast."

"Thanks, Miri, but I'm more interested in the weather for Canaan."

"The average temperature for Canada this time of year is 56 degrees Fahrenheit, 13.33333 degrees Celsius. Do you have a particular Canadian city in mind?"

"No, not Canada. Canaan," Max said. "As in

the Torah. I want to go back four thousand years and visit Abraham, Sarah, and the angels—from Genesis."

"Oh, well, that's a different story," Miri said. "It's hot there. Be prepared to sweat buckets. Are you sure you don't want to go to Canada?"

"I'm sure."

"Okay. 2000 BCE. Land of Canaan. Abraham and Sarah's tent. Got it."

# Chapter 4

# Max Lands Somewhere Hot and Smelly

It was a bumpy ride, and Max landed in the hot desert with a thud. Was there a prayer to thank God for traveling safely through time? Max didn't know, so he said Hamotzi again.

Wow, he thought. There was sand everywhere! "This sure would be nicer with an ocean and a miniature golf course," Max said to Miri.

"Canada has three oceans and hundreds of mini-golf courses," Miri replied.

Max also noticed that the desert was a bit smelly. His time machine had landed right next to three camels and a goat.

"Pee-yew." Max hid his time machine behind a thorny bush.

"Look over there," Miri said. "There's a man sitting on a beach blanket."

The man had a long beard and a long white tunic. As Max crept closer to gain a better view, he saw three

robed men walking by the man's tent. One was tall and looked like he had just swallowed a lemon. One was short and walked with a bounce in his step. And one—with a little gold ring in his left ear—seemed easily distracted by passing lizards and dragonflies.

The man from the tent ran to meet the sweaty people. For an old man, he ran pretty fast. Then he bowed all the way to the ground.

"I wonder why he's doing that," Max said.

"Bowing is a sign of respect," Miri said. "That, or he is trying out a new dance move."

Max crept even closer.

"Friends, if it is all right with you, do not rush ahead and pass me by," said the man from the tent. "Let me bring you some water and bathe your feet. You can rest under my tree. And let me get you something to eat. My wife Sarah makes a brisket to die for. Believe me, you won't be disappointed. I'm Abraham, by the way. And you?"

"I'm Simcha," said the cheerful visitor. "This is Ragzoni. The one looking at the dragonfly is Chalomi. Please excuse him. Sometimes his head's in the clouds." Just like Emma, Max thought.

"Are you sure we won't be a bother?" Ragzoni asked.

"No bother at all!" Abraham said. "After all, this is a land flowing with milk and honey."

The three visitors sheepishly looked at their dusty feet.

"No dairy products, please," Simcha said.

Chalomi pointed to Ragzoni's tummy. "He doesn't do so good with milk."

"Gas," Ragzoni said glumly.

"Understood," Abraham said. "No dairy for you!"

This was amazing! Based on what Abraham said to the visitors, Max was pretty sure he had landed in the right place. Just as they had learned in class, Abraham didn't seem to know that he was talking to angels. Max checked for any wing-shaped lumps under their robes. Nope. Maybe Emma was right, and the angels really were like Transformers. It was time for Max to introduce himself and see if he could find out.

"Shalom!" Max said. "I come in peace!"

"OY! A golem! What's he wearing? Are those wings?" Simcha asked.

"And what's on his eyes? Is he some kind of giant bug?" Chalomi asked. "Maybe he's a locust!"

"Naah, worse than that. Check out his sandals!

Looks like he's from the land of the Moabites! Shoo, Moabite, shoo!" Ragzoni yelled.

Max froze. This was definitely not going according to plan.

Abraham looked at Max from head to toe. Then he smiled.

"He's just a little boy wearing funny clothes. What's your name, little boy?" Abraham asked.

"Max."

"Interesting name," Abraham said. "So, Max, are you hungry maybe? You like brisket? Come, let me wash your feet and give you water to drink."

Abraham removed Max's blinking sneakers.

"Hmmm," Abraham said. "I'm guessing you're not from around here."

"Not exactly." Max's heart was beating fast. Maybe Abraham would send him away because he was not from Canaan. Instead, Abraham began to wash Max's feet. Max found this very relaxing.

"Why are you washing my feet?" Max asked.

"You've come a long way and it's hot. Your feet hurt, no? This is how we welcome people we don't know well. It's also how we honor God."

Max's feet were ticklish, so he started to giggle. This made Simcha giggle. By the time Abraham had finished washing Max's feet, *everyone* was giggling—except for Ragzoni, who still looked like he had just swallowed a lemon.

A pretty lady peeked out from an opening in the tent. "So, Abraham, darling, what's with the giggling? Did someone tell a joke?"

Abraham blushed.

"Forgive me, Sarah. These are our guests. I hope you don't mind, but I've invited them all for lunch. One of them, Max, has ticklish feet."

Sarah smiled. "Well, Max with Ticklish Feet, welcome to our home. My name is Sarah."

She turned to Abraham.

"Abe, dear, could I have a word with you inside the tent?"

# Chapter 5

# Max Makes a Discovery

**M**ax knew it was rude to spy on people, but he couldn't help himself. He crouched behind the tent to listen to Abraham and Sarah. Maybe Sarah wasn't happy to have three men and a little boy stay for lunch on such short notice. What if she just wanted to give them some juice and cookies and send them on their way?

What Max heard surprised him.

"Abraham, you have our guests sitting on an old

camel blanket? Where are your manners, dear?"
Sarah asked. "Quick, fetch the pillows! And did you
ask them if they have any food allergies?"

"One of our visitors can't have dairy," Abraham
said. "It gives him gas."

"Well, then, my famous cottage cheese is out of
the question," Sarah said. "I know! I'll serve them a
brisket! Abe, darling, don't just stand there. Go tell the
servant to finish preparing the cow. I'll make bread.
Oy! So little time! So much to do."

Max returned to the blanket just as Abraham was bringing out some fluffy pillows.

"Please forgive me," Abraham said. "My wife reminded me that I forgot these."

"Such comfortable pillows!" Simcha said.

"Like floating on a cloud!" Ragzoni said.

"I'm in heaven!" Chalomi said.

Ragzoni quickly shook his head at Chalomi.

"Not that I would know, of course, what heaven is like," Chalomi added.

Abraham did not seem to understand what the angels were talking about, but Max did. Now Max was sure he was dealing with angels! But where were they hiding their wings?

"Max, what's with the staring?" Chalomi asked. "Did I spill something on my robe?"

"He's such a slob," Ragzoni sighed. "We can't take him anywhere."

Abraham looked at Chalomi from head to toe. "I don't see anything."

Neither could Max. These angels sure were mysterious.

The pillows were so comfortable that Max and the angels took a nap while Sarah and the servant finished cooking the meal. Max awoke to the sight of brisket and the aroma of warm, golden bread, unsure of how long he had slept.

"We waited for you," Simcha said, smiling. The

meal reminded Max of Shabbat dinner with his parents, his favorite time of the week.

Max and the angels ate with gusto. Or, at least, that's what seemed to happen.

"Excuse me," Max whispered, "but did you really eat the food, or were you just pretending to eat it?"

Simcha winked. "It's a mystery," he said. "What do you think, Max?"

Max looked at Abraham and Sarah, who were smiling at him. Suddenly, Max realized that it didn't matter if the angels could eat or if they had wings.

"What's really important is that by serving us a meal, Abraham and Sarah have treated four perfect strangers like family. They've shown us how we should live our lives," he said. "Right?"

"You're a pretty smart kid," Simcha said.

"Especially for a Moabite," Ragzoni said.

Then all three angels burped loudly.

"Is this what angels do?" Max whispered.

"No," Chalomi said. "It's what people in the desert do to show appreciation for a good meal."

Following the angels' example, Max did something he could never do at home without being sent to his room.

"BURRRRRRP!!!"

Sarah and Abraham laughed. Max smiled sheepishly.

"Thank you for the compliment," Sarah said. "You're all welcome to visit us anytime. I'm just sorry I have no leftovers for you. I guess I should have used a bigger cow."

"Thank you, dear Sarah, for your hospitality,"

Simcha said. He winked at Max. "Believe me, I couldn't have *eaten* another bite."

Abraham helped Max to his feet.

"You're a funny boy, Max, and you have a good heart. I hope you'll come back and visit us. And if any strangers pass by your own tent, I hope you, too, will try to make them feel welcome."

Max thought of Emma and how she was new in class. Instead of ignoring her, maybe he could have asked what she thought of his time machine drawing. Would she forgive him for insulting her? Could they still become friends? He had to find out.

Max hugged everyone and then ran back to his

time machine. The camels were gone and the goat was snoring.

"Miri, let's go home," he said. "I need to fix something."

# Chapter 6

# Friends?

**O**n Monday morning, before the school bell rang, Max spied Emma hanging from the monkey bars. Her floppy hat was on the ground. As usual, no one was playing with her.

"Do you know you're upside-down?"

"Yes," Emma said. "Sometimes the world looks better this way."

"How was your weekend?"

"Quiet," Emma said. "On Saturday night, after

Shabbat, my mom and I saw the Big Dipper through my telescope."

"Cool," Max said. "Ummm . . . see any angels?"

"No, it was kind of cloudy. Did *you*?"

"Maybe." Max smiled.

Emma hopped off the monkey bars. After putting her hat firmly on her head, she placed her hands on her hips and glared at Max.

"Are you making fun of me?" she asked.

"I have a time machine."

"Oh, right. And *I'm* the weird one?"

"No, really." Max then shared the story of his trip to the desert.

"So they're not Transformers, and they don't eat tuna fish?" Emma asked.

"Like I said, I don't know," Max said. "The only thing I know for sure is that they really seem to like brisket and pillows and that they're—"

"Mysterious," Emma said.

"Exactly," Max said.

"Did this *really* happen?"

"Do you want to—"

Just then the bell rang.

"Do I want to what?" Emma asked.

Max pointed to the kids lining up to enter the building. "No time. Recess?"

"Sure," Emma said. "Let's meet on the steps."

As usual, class began with morning prayers.

"Eitan, please put the plane away. And Max, please stop looking at the clock," Mrs. Mooshky said.

"Emma, nice job leading services."

Emma did a little happy dance as she returned to her seat.

"Okay, class, let's learn a little Torah," Mrs. Mooshky said. "Does anyone know anything about the Exodus from Egypt?"

As he thought about meeting Emma on the steps, Max couldn't help but fidget and look at the clock again.

Emma waved her hand wildly and popped out of her seat. "Ooh! Ooh! I know! I know!"

For what seemed like forty years, Max listened to Emma drone on about the Exodus story. He only stopped fidgeting when Emma described how God split the Red Sea in two.

Max raised his hand. "Mrs. Mooshky, do you think there were any angels when God split the Red Sea?"

"That's a wonderful question, Max," Mrs. Mooshky said. "Honestly, I don't recall—but I would like to think there are usually angels floating about when God performs miracles."

Max couldn't remember the last time Mrs. Mooshky had praised him in front of the whole class. Even better, she offered Max hope that he might see some angels again! Maybe Mrs. Mooshky wasn't so bad after all.

Just then, the recess bell rang. Max and Emma were the first kids out of their seats.

As the others raced to the monkey bars, the slide, and the swings, Max and Emma sat on the steps to the school entrance. Then Max asked what was probably the most important question of his whole life. It was so important that he scrunched his eyes closed to ask it.

"So, Emma, do you want to maybe come over to my house on Sunday and play?"

Max opened one eye and peeked at Emma.

Emma twirled several loose curls of her frizzy red hair, adjusted her floppy hat, looked at the clouds, studied her pink sneakers for what seemed like forever, and finally nodded—*yes*.

Max sighed. It felt good to be forgiven. It felt even better to have a friend.

"Do you really think God parted the Red Sea?" he asked. This time he looked at Emma with his eyes wide open. "Wanna come with me to find out?"

"Can I bring my poodle?"

Emma smiled at her new friend.
And Max smiled right back.

# A Note for Families

Imagine that you have just moved to a new neighborhood and don't know anyone in your class, on the playground, or in your synagogue. How would that feel?

Or imagine that someone new in town asks to play with you. Would you give that person a chance? Does it matter what other kids might think?

Max may not be so good at building friendships, but he does know how to build things out of cardboard and spare parts—including a time machine! When he travels to biblical times, he discovers what it feels like to be the "new kid on the block" (or in the tent).

It takes imagination to create a time machine and courage to visit the unknown. It also takes imagination to build new friendships and courage to welcome newcomers with an open heart.

What are some things you might do to make a new friend feel more welcome?